THE
BLAH

JACK
KENT

PARENTS' MAGAZINE PRESS • NEW YORK

To Mary Lou

Once upon a time
there was a Blah . . .
a nothing . . . a nobody . . .
named Billy.

"I'm just a Blah!" Billy told
his mother.

"Yes, dear," said his mother,
who was busy and wasn't
really listening.

That's how it is,
being a Blah.
Nobody listens
to you.

Billy sat down on the floor
and drew a picture.
It was a picture of himself.
It was a picture of a Blah.
A sort of nothing
with a sad expression.

Billy's older brother, Richard,
came hurrying around the corner
and jostled Billy and stepped on
one of his crayons. The green one,
Billy's favorite.

Richard hardly noticed
as he hurried on his way.

That's how it is, being a Blah.
Nobody notices you.

"I'll bet I'm not the only Blah
in the world," Billy said to
himself. "I'll bet there are
lots of Blahs."

And he drew some.

"I'll bet if all the Blahs got together, folks would notice us then!" Billy thought.

He drew orange ones and red ones and blue ones. But of course there weren't any green ones because Richard had smashed the green crayon.

Billy was King of the Blahs.
He was leading his troops
into battle.

While looking for a battle
to lead his troops into, the King
saw a very strange sight.

Some people were upside-down
in a patch of daisies.

"We were jostled into the daisy
patch by the Terrible, Awful
Jostler named Richard who lives
in the castle on the hill,"
the people explained.

"We'll have to do something about that!" said the King of the Blahs, as he helped them up and dusted them off.

Farther on they saw some children
who were crying so hard that
their tears had formed a small lake,
which a duck and a fish and a
polliwog named Sam were swimming in.

"It's the Terrible, Awful Jostler named Richard who lives in the castle on the hill," they explained. "He smashed our crayons!"

"We'll have to do something
about that!" said the King
of the Blahs, as he dried
their eyes and wiped their noses.

The Blahs marched
up the hill to the castle.
They knocked politely
and then broke down
the door and went in.

The King bowed to the Jostler
and said, "How do you do?"
and challenged him to a
jostling match.

It was a horrible
thing to watch.

For a while the Terrible, Awful
Jostler was winning, but the King
gathered all his strength for
one colossal jostle.

It sent the Jostler rolling
down the stairs, out the door,
down the hill, and into the
lake of tears!

While the Jostler was trying to
get the water out of his ears
and the polliwog named Sam
out of his pocket . . .

the Blahs searched his castle
and stomped every crayon
they found.

The dripping-wet, black and blue
Jostler begged for mercy.

"Stop!" he said.
"Stop what you're doing!"

"Yes, yes. Quite so," said the
King of the Blahs, who was busy
and wasn't really listening.
"Lovely day for crayon stomping."

"I said stop what you're doing
and get ready for supper!"
Billy's mother said. "Pay some
attention to me!

"Sometimes you act as if you don't
even know I'm around," said Mother.
"I feel like a . . . a . . ."

"A Blah?" asked Billy.

"That's just what I feel like!"
said Mother.

"You can be the Queen of the Blahs,"
Billy said.

And he kissed his mother
and went to wash up for supper.